Drowned In Dusk

Wolf With Ink

anvi saini

Copyright © --All Rights Reserved.

Made with love on the Notion Press Platform

www.notionpress.com

For, those who were lost,

but never truly gone

Contents

Chapter I

The Cellar

I walked down the night street just for a walk and to sit near the lake. The warm air hit me as I stepped outside, the bright streetlight stinging my eyes for a brief moment, I hadn't been outside in months.   It was really cold in the November winter, the cold which I like the cold due to which the air smells great. The dryness of the air, it's so calming. Just a normal night in the city, the roads are empty, it looks peaceful, the streetlights, the grey sky, and, the ethereal moon. Yes, I pay attention and notice more than a few other people around me, some people are receptive towards a few things while others are not. There might be many people like me in the universe, everybody has their own natural skills and talents that are equally important in keeping the world balanced, so it's beneficial for everyone if you just keep doing you. It's always important to remember to love and accept yourself for who you are. By the way, I'm Rose, my new mom gave me this name. A girl who lives a strange life. Kidnapped as a child and raised by someone else. Someone who made their own assumptions about how a child lived. But anyhow, they love me, isn't it? It's been eleven years. After me, they continued to kidnap the other children in the same way. And the cops have never reached to them.

But yes they have given me a home. Should I call it home? Home to me isn't necessarily a physical thing, it can be your mind, an experience, a place, or a person too. Where you find inner peace. For me, it's a place I haven't touched, a sleep I haven't slept. A dream I have often. A place I can be told I cannot go. I do have a family there waiting for me looking down over me. I long to go there in my time. I'm afraid of being turned away regardless of how much I pray or how much I say. Home? I've been homeless since birth

There were many times when I had considered death an option. To close my eyes, accept my fate and, fall into a deep peace that I'd never been able to obtain while living. It was a feeling I have had, but unfortunately, *a feeling* it remained.

There is no such thing as a great suffering, great regret, great memory. Everything is forgotten after a while, even a great love. That's what's sad about life, and also what's wonderful about it. There is only a way of looking at things, which can change anytime. Change is constant just like growth. I believe growth and change are synonyms. Nothing is real, even a fact is a perception built by a human mind. We are just taught in a way to accept. That's what makes life so interesting. But downgrade our worth.

I have never felt so worthless or disposable, never so wretched and cold. For hours I would have no emotion, only an urge to move fast;

then all at once I'd be on the floor, shaking with a grief that bled from my bones. Days became weeks and weeks become months, and in every single moment of every single day I tell myself that ~~I'm a child, I don't have to be stronger, I need to be safe~~ I need to be strong to keep myself safe. emptiness still comes like an ambush.

Do you ever sit and listen to your breath, feel your bones in your muscles, try to hear your pulses beating in the lowest frequencies. Or touch your scars. I'm not talking about your mental state, I'm talking about feeling your physical self. To know, where does it ache? I usually get the sudden urge to feel it. I scream, I feel, I suffer. Only my enigma interests me, and more than anything, I search for myself in my great void.

It's happening to me, it starts as a mere tingle in my knuckles, before the strange sensation- a kind of prickling, like a sleeping limb waking up, began to climb. It scales the rough, raise edges of scar that weave across my forearm, then, as it reaches the curve of my elbow, the prickling suddenly sharpens. It flares into a burn, deep and scorching, raging through me. It felt like my arm is being consumed by the hottest fire, like the Beast had it gripped in it's great, terrible, flaming mouth.

I let out a sharp cry and clutched my arm to my chest.

Several people on the busy restaurant patio turned in my direction, their gazes both curious and concerned.

Ignoring them, I squeezed my eyes shut and tried to focus on thoughts of cool breezes and rushing streams, trying to imagine the water quenching the invisible flames. And kept saying inside my mind "the world is pretty" like a phrase or utterance used to feel calm

This is all in your head, I reminded myself as I tried to wilt the pain away. *It's not real. It's not real.*

But, damn, *did it ever feel real.*

After several moments- that seemed to stretch on like hours- the pain finally began to recede.

It ebbed away in waves until the scar was once again numb, lulled back into sleep. With a sigh of relief, I loosened my fingers, leaving bands of white where they had pressed hard into the angry red.

I start walking towards home.

By the way, I live in a cellar. That's the home they gave me, with me there lived a girl with the name Rhyse. Julie (my mother) said that Rhyse is my sister. But I don't know where is she, haven't seen her in a week. Since the past years she hasn't spoken a word. I never saw her mouth open. She never went out of the cellar and stayed in one corner. For the first time in eight years she is not there when I enter the room. I'm hoping she is safe wherever she is. I miss her. I have seen her grow up. I feel torn when I see the room empty.

Rhyse   please   come   back.

Julie doesn't know about Rhyse isn't here yet. She hasn't opened the cellar since a week or served us food. I certainly know she wont check it for two days more. Julie would burn me in the dead fire if I go out of the cellar without permission of her, Jace or Kiva. Jace is my father. Kiva is Julie's sister. But haha I cannot surely speak about the relations because this is *just* what I was told when I was kidnapped.

Anyways I take the risk smartly and just rarely go for a walk like this 'cause unlike Rhyse I have always wanted to grieve less and escape fast. Magnus who lives in the next house near the cellar helped me in getting a spare key for myself.

But mostly I don't go. Sometimes a week can pass. I don't go outside. I keep my secrets to myself, let dirt accumulate beneath my nails.

Sometimes suffering is just suffering. It doesn't make you stronger. It doesn't build character. It only hurts.

Honestly, I can even run away from here to my family in any moment with my braveness but the point is I won't have anywhere to go. I don't know where is my family, I don't know if they even search for me or are they alive.. Is this really the world.. shall I grieve…or shall I hope… shall I.. die.. shall I drown… shall I burn them.. was I raised without love? Or was I born unloveable..?

Great loneliness, profound isolation, a cataclysmic overpowering sense of being misunderstood. When does that kind of deep feeling just stop? Where does it go? At seven, the world ended over and over and over again. But here I am, I am young and optimistic.

~~To be so young feels like a kind of self-violence.~~

Sometimes I wish to melt the steel and drink it to fill the void inside of me. Let it burn through my veins, as if the molten metal could mend the emptiness within.

I reach to the cellar and instantly open the door and get in. its so dark, scary and lonely in here. But peaceful than the noisy streets. I feel hungry, I haven't eaten anything since morning. My ribs echo hunger, a feast of emptiness served for days. I felt a rush of vomit through my throat. My stomach makes a weird sound and I feel pain in entire body. I drink water from the tap endlessly and tell myself to wait and have patience.. I lie down on floor to sleep and close my eyes to distract myself.

Julie left me for a week without giving me food, I don't know what must have happened to Rhyse if she was here. But to me, usually Magnus gets me food. He is a kind old man. If I'm most grateful to anyone then its him.

But I don't like to take help from him every time, he's old and I have always been a self - respect cautious, once I was inspired by a girl in a story I read in kindergarten, my real mum read it to me and since then I wanted to be brave. Well yeah, my mother was thousand times better than Julie, but doesn't deserve to compare 'cause I know Julie is my kidnapper. I remember thinking my father was mean but knowing he was good hearted and then thinking he was good hearted but knowing he was   mean..

I was kidnapped when I was just seven. I don't know my correct age today but I've grown up.

I always counted the days and to my seven year old math it's been eleven years. Seven plus eleven is equal to eighteen. So am I eighteen. Nobody taught me but I did. I remember Julie told me Rhyse was five, so now she is sixteen. Where would she be…

My chest suddenly aches and a tear flows as I lie on the other side of the floor and close my eyes oncc again. For the first time in my life I'm missing someone…

I wonder is there anybody to miss me either.. does Rhyse miss me..

I am so tired that even the mere act of inhaling and exhaling right now feels like a thousand knives piercing my bones.. I feel my silence is so desperate to be heard. It's a loud voice which is on mute.

Chapter II

Cerebral Hush

The water was black, endless, a silent grave with no bottom.

It wrapped around me like a second skin, crushing, dragging me down into its depths. I kicked, thrashed, reached for the surface, but where was it? No light broke through the abyss. No direction, no escape. Just endless, suffocating blackness.

The cold crept into my bones, turning my veins to ice. My lungs burned, my limbs ached, like a pressure of blood carving through muscle and marrow, a slow, creeping death, how much longer could I hold on before the dark swallowed me whole?

Am I going to die here?

Panic surged through me, raw and sharp. I kicked harder, pushing against the weight of the abyss

Something brushed my leg.

I froze. My pulse pounded in my ears. Again, it slithered against my back—slick, slow, alive. I turned, but the darkness hid everything.

Then, without warning it struck. A cold, slimy coil wrapped around my throat, tightening, choking.

Body convulsing, vision fracturing,

And then my eyes flew open.

No water. No abyss.

Just the solid ground beneath me. I lay there, my breath raged, my pulse in wild storm. My skin was still cold. My heart still raced.

Just a dream, I whispered. But in the silence, it felt like the darkness had followed me back.

I wake up instantly in fear, I have always been a light sleeper and it's something I despise.

It's rare that I get dreams but when I get they are the scariest, like a demon lighting a matchstick inside my mouth.

I always wished a genie to be the most powerful entity of the world until once he appeared in my dream and trapped me in its lamp. The reason wasn't that he trapped me but I realized how lonely he must be and still fulfill wishes of others. He's a kind man. And some things are better to be left underrated and out of people's vision because humans ruin whatever they see.

every single sound- the drop of a penny, a whisper in the hallway, is enough to wake me. I reach over aimlessly to turn on the light. Once I hit the switch, the whole room is silenced again, and I'm plagued with only one question: what day is it?

this happens more often than you think: a brief, blissful moment, where I'm unsure of every thing.. haven't you ever felt that way? Lost in a space-time continuum, only truly certain of what day is it. Time is just a social construct, after all. Our perception of time is subjective.

I realize soon, that it's Wednesday. Well, how docs that even matter to me?

I get up and stare at myself in the mirror, the red eyes, messed up hair and, a knife kept on the floor. Magnus must have left the knife when he brought me an apple yesterday morning.

The knife feels heavy in my hands, passing between my fingers with increased accuracy. The stainless steel is warm as it shakes, prompted to do so by my nerves. Traitorous, a growl emerges from the deepest pits of my stomach. Clawing its way through my insides. It demands more, but more is going to kill me.

It reminds me of a feeling I have had once before. When I was around thirteen years old.

It was a point in my life that I wanted to stop, quit, and leave everything behind just to disappear.

I believe reincarnation is undoubtedly what happens. I think we are souls or you could say spirits inside human bodies.

A few years back, at the age of thirteen. when I woke up I went near the drawer to get something to drink and took a caffeine pill as I usually did. Shortly after that, I felt a very sharp pain right in the middle of my chest. I turned around to look at Rhyse as I opened my mouth and signaled that I needed something to drink as I couldn't breathe with this unbearable pain.

As all this was happening I was looking toward the wall and my vision went out. The way it went has been very clear to me to this day as it is a life-changing moment that I will never forget.

All of my vision that I could see started to zoom out into a dark black tunnel, then when it got to almost a milli meter in diameter it just burst into this fine horizontal line before all just vanished before me. What I felt was that something heavy and cold was evaporating from my physical body; I would describe the sensation like when you remove the nail paint and you feel the nail paint remover cold and heavy on your nails while it evaporates.

At this time now I know that my physical sight had been gone but it was as if I could still see unconsciously or perhaps kind of like an out-of-body experience. That is just when I turned towards the door. I could remember that all I was thinking was how I needed some fresh air. At this point, I took a step towards the open door, and that's just when I had collapsed.

The experience then suddenly changed.
I wasn't dead, as my consciousness was still there, I wasn't alive as I was no longer in my body. I was just simply being. I was an eternal force. An energy beyond explanation. It was like floating in the air.

I was no longer seeing the world, I wasn't even seeing black. I was in a place bright as white. It was peaceful and perhaps heavenly.

The thing that I remembered the most was a sense of selfishness if I can truly put it into words. As I remembered my life, it didn't have much feeling of worth any more. I felt like everything was perfect and just the way it should be. In this state, I had no care, no compassion, no fear, no reason to want to come back to this life. not worried about family, not worried about missing them or the sadness they would feel. I was selfish and didn't care, I didn't even have feelings anymore. In all senses of the word, it was euphoria.

Throughout this entire ordeal, I did not see ghosts, past family members or past friends. I didn't see God, I didn't even see the Devil. There was no heaven or hell as far as I could tell.

All of a sudden it was like a bomb of awakening, I opened my eyes with confusion as to where I was, and I started to realize that I was looking at the floor with my drool falling to hit the floor. My eyelash was tangled and felt little heavy, and I felt a bit more confused as I started to realize that I was coming back into my body.

This feeling of life suddenly changed as I realized I have a huge sensitivity all over. I had a heavy head for a few weeks that I hadn't even realized that I had suppressed. I had pain in my leg that I realized I had for the past week. I had a pain in my back that I only just realized I had for the past three days. It was amazing the heaviness I then felt I had to endure just to carry this body around every day.

At this time in my life, I was suddenly enlightened. I realized that life is all about pain and suffering.
I have a clear understanding now that while we make our choices to try to find a better afterlife.

It was now more clear.

I have never been religious before and I was not such a bad kid either... I was always finding flaws in the teaching of science and religion.

This experience has not made me to be much of a different person. I'm still a very morally ethical person. I am still not quite so religious. I'm still not an atheist or anything of the like. While my religious beliefs are complicated it would need an entire explanation for another time.

What I can say is that this experience has given me a bit of understanding that if there is a heaven and hell. Then this material life would be hell and the afterlife would be heaven, as it is euphoria.

Since then I have never feared death nor pain and I am always ready to go back. It's a place of being. A place of knowledge. A place of wisdom. A place where there is no hate or even love.

One of the reasons why I believe Rhyse will come back.

Chapter III

Rhyse

The cellar is quieter than ever. The silence sits thick, curling in the air like dust disturbed by ghosts. I press my fingers to the cold, uneven stone of the wall, feeling its roughness bite into my skin. My heart hammers.

Rhyse is still not here.

The thought seeps into me, slow and heavy, like ink bleeding through fabric. It has been more than a week. My ribs ache from hunger, but it is not the emptiness in my stomach that makes me feel weak, it is the hollowness in my chest. A strange ache that has no name.

Where is she?

The dim glow of the small, rusted bulb overhead flickers for a second, sending shadows stretching across the walls. They look almost alive, twisting, writhing, like silent whispers taking form. I pull my knees to my chest, the cold biting through my skin.

Julie hasn't checked the cellar. Not once.

The thought slithers in, unwelcome. If she hasn't checked, then where is Rhyse? Did she leave? Was she taken? Or…

I shake the thought away.

No. No, she's not dead.

I don't know how I know this, but I do. Maybe it's because death has a presence, I've felt it before, that heavy, consuming void. But Rhyse is not in it. She is somewhere, breathing, living. I just don't know where.

I reach near the and pull out the small notebook I keep hidden. It's nothing much, just scraps of thoughts, scribbles of words I am afraid to say out loud. I flip to the last page.

"Rhyse, where are you?"

The words sit there, hollow and unanswered.

I take the pen, my fingers trembling slightly, and begin to write again.

"You never speak, but I have always heard you. The way your breath hitches when you're afraid, the way your fingers curl when you sleep, as if you're holding onto something no one else can see. I hear you in the silence, in the way your presence filled this empty space without needing a single word. But now… Now the silence is too loud, too empty. Where are you?"

I let the pen drop, rubbing my eyes with the back of my hand. The air is heavy, pressing against my ribs.

Then—

A sound.

Faint. Distant. But real.

I freeze, my breath catching in my throat. It comes again, a shuffle, a creak, something brushing against the walls of the house above. My heart pounds. My fingers grip the cold steel of the knife Magnus left me.

And then—

A whisper.

The cellar door yawns open, and there she is

Rhyse.

Her skin is pale, her dark hair tangled like vines twisted in a storm. She stands in the dim glow of the moonlight spilling through the cracks in the ceiling, her eyes wide and unreadable. She doesn't move. Doesn't speak.

But she's alive.

Relief claws up my throat, raw and desperate. I step forward, reaching for her

"Rhyse!"

She flinches. And then—silence.

Her hands tremble, but there's something in them, something fierce and unbreakable. She grips my wrist with fingers like iron hooks, her nails digging into my skin.

"We have to go."

A knife twists in my stomach.

"What? Where have you…"

"Now."

Her voice is sharp as a blade, cutting through the thick, rotting air.

"Before she comes."

Julie.

Her name alone feels like a fist pressing against my ribs, squeezing the breath from my lungs.

The stairs above us creak.

Slow. Heavy. Calculated.

My blood turns to ice.

"They know."

The words are barely a whisper, but they crack something deep inside me.

A shadow shifts at the top of the stairs, and then,

Jace.

His frame blocks the doorway, tall and unmoving. The dim light casts deep shadows across his face, his eyes gleaming with something unreadable.

Behind him, Julie emerges from the darkness.

She isn't alone.

Kiva steps out beside her, arms crossed, lips curled into something that isn't quite a smile.

And then I see it

the knife in Julie's hand.

She tilts her head, her expression almost… amused.

"I was wondering when you'd finally grow a spine, Rose," she murmurs. "But I never thought Rhyse would be the one to lead you."

My pulse pounds in my ears.

"You knew," I whisper.

Julie's smile widens, teeth glinting like a wolf's. "Of course, sweetheart. Did you really think I wouldn't?"

Jace steps closer, his boots thudding against the wooden floor. His voice is smooth, deep, soaked in something dark and unmovable.

"Did you really think we'd let you leave?"

Something cold coils in my stomach. A feeling I've had before, the one that whispers *you are nothing. You are a thing, a belonging, a body without ownership.*

Julie exhales, her fingers brushing the edge of the blade. "You always wanted to know why we took you, didn't you?"

I don't answer. I can't.

She steps closer, lowering her voice, as if sharing a secret.

"We didn't steal you, Rose. We saved you."

The world tilts.

A laugh.. low and sharp.. spills from her lips. "Your parents weren't searching for you. They were selling you."

My breath stops. My heart slams against my ribs, wild and caged.

"No," I choke out.

"Yes," Julie croons. "Your mother didn't cry when we took you. Your father didn't fight. Because they knew they'd get their money either way."

I want to scream. I want to break something. I want this to be a lie.

But then I see Rhyse's face.

She isn't shocked.

She knew.

A sharp crack of thunder shakes the walls, no, not thunder. A door slamming open.

And then, a voice.. deep, commanding, unfamiliar.

"POLICE! HANDS WHERE WE CAN SEE THEM!"

The air erupts.

Julie's face twists in rage. Jace spins toward the sound, reaching for something under his jacket

A gunshot shatters the silence.

The impact sends Julie stumbling, her mouth parting in shock. Blood blooms across her stomach, staining her dress like a wilted rose.

She falls.

Jace lunges, but before he can move, two officers slam him to the ground.

The world is chaos.

Shouts. Heavy footsteps. The sound of metal cuffs clicking into place.

And through it all

Rhyse grips my hand.

Her voice is trembling when she whispers:

"It's over, Rose."

I don't know if she's right.

But for the first time in eleven years..

I want to believe her.

Julie is on the floor, blood spreading beneath her like ink staining paper. Her lips part, but no sound escapes. Her fingers tremble as they press against the wound, as if she can hold herself together with sheer will.

Jace is pinned to the ground, his face pressed against the cold floor, hands twisted behind his back. He doesn't fight. He doesn't beg. He just laughs.. low and bitter, like he knows something we don't.

The officers move quickly, their voices sharp, their commands clear. Kiva stands frozen, her expression unreadable.

And then, her eyes meet mine.

A shiver crawls up my spine.

She isn't afraid. She isn't angry. She is… smiling.

Not a real smile.

Something calm. Knowing. Expectant.

As if this was all part of a plan.

A cold whisper slips from her lips.

"You really thought this was the end?"

The words sink into my bones like ice.

A second later, the lights flicker.

Once. Twice.

Then, darkness.

The cellar is swallowed whole. The shouts turn into frantic calls. Heavy boots shuffle against the ground. Someone curses. A gun is cocked.

I can't breathe. I can't see.

Then,

A sharp, searing pain slices across my arm.

I scream.

The lights flash back on

Julie is gone.

Jace is gone.

Kiva is gone.

All that remains is a single, fresh wound across my arm, blood dripping onto the cold floor. A warning. A mark.

I clutch my arm, my breath ragged. Rhyse grabs me, her fingers tight around my wrist. Her face is pale, her eyes wide with something that looks a lot like fear.

The officers scramble, shouting into their radios, demanding backup, ordering searches.

But I already know.

They won't find them.

Julie, Jace, and Kiva, they planned this.

They let us think we won.

And now, they are *hunting* us.

A strange silence settles over the cellar, like the house itself is holding its breath.

Rhyse grips my wrist tighter, her fingers cold and unsteady. Her eyes flicker to my wound, then back to my face. "They planned this" she whispers.

I swallow hard. I already know.

"They let us think we won" I murmur. "And now, they're hunting us."

A shudder runs through Rhyse. For years, she stayed silent. For years, she sat in the corner of this cellar like a wilted flower, never speaking, never moving. But now, her silence has shattered. And somehow, that terrifies me more than the darkness itself.

My eyes fall to the ground. Near the old wooden crates, something catches my attention, a single white lily, wilted and dry, forgotten in the cracks of the stone.

A flower that never had sunlight. That never had a chance to bloom.

I don't know why, but the sight of it makes my chest tighten.

Are we just flowers trapped in a garden which is not a garden?

I shake the thought away and turn to Rhyse. "Let's go."

We step over the blood, over the broken past,
and walk toward the light.

But deep in my bones, I know

Julie, Jace, and Kiva will return.

And when they do, they will not come as
people.

they will come as a storm.

Chapter IV

Wilted Truths

The night air is thick, pressing against my skin like unseen hands. I can still feel the weight of the cellar on my back, the scent of old stone and dust still clinging to my breath.

Rhyse and I don't speak as we move. The world outside feels unnatural, like I've stepped into a painting, something beautiful, but not quite real. The city lights flicker above us, artificial stars in a world where the sky doesn't care to shine.

But inside me, the hush has returned.

That eerie, creeping silence, slipping into the cracks of my ribs. A phantom whisper. A presence I can't see but can always feel. Cerebral hush.

I try to drown it out, but it lingers.

"You think you're free, but you're just a flower in a glass box, waiting to wilt."

My breath catches. The voice is not my own. It has no body, no face. It is a part of me, but also something else.

"No" I whisper under my breath. "Not anymore."

But the voice only laughs.

"Julie is still watching, Rose. Jace is still out there. Kiva is waiting."

A cold shiver curls around my spine. I clutch my wounded arm, feeling the pulse beneath my skin. I am bleeding, but I am breathing. And as long as I am breathing, I am not dead yet.

Rhyse suddenly tugs at my sleeve. "We're here."

I blink, pulling myself back into the present. We're standing in front of an old, abandoned house, windows shattered, vines creeping through cracks, as if nature itself is trying to take back what was stolen.

"This is where they are" Rhyse murmurs.

I don't ask who. I already know.

We step inside, and the air changes.

It is thick with something unseen. Something alive.

And then, I see them.

Lily. Clover. Daisy. Dahlia.

They sit in the dim light, their figures barely illuminated by the dying glow of a candle. Their eyes snap toward us, sharp and searching. Not scared. Not welcoming. Just watching.

For a moment, no one speaks. The silence is heavy, but it's different from the hush in my head. This silence is shared, an unspoken grief, a breath we have all been holding.

Then, Lily stands.

She is taller than I expected, her dark curls cascading over her shoulders like ivy on abandoned walls. Her voice is soft, but there's steel beneath it.

"You're one of us" she says.

I don't know how to respond.

Dahlia tilts her head, studying me. "Rhyse said you'd come," she murmurs. "She said you'd bring a storm with you."

A flicker of unease twists in my stomach. I glance at Rhyse, but she doesn't meet my gaze.

"You knew about them?" I ask.

Rhyse nods slowly. "I always knew."

The betrayal is small, but it stings.

"And Julie?" Lily asks.

"She's gone" I say. "But she won't stay gone."

A shadow passes over Clover's face. She leans forward, fingers curling into her dress. "Then we don't have much time."

My chest tightens. "Time for what?"

Daisy exhales, her voice barely above a whisper.

"To finish what we started."

The air thickens.

Something about this moment feels too perfect, too staged, as if I have walked into a scene that has played out before.

And then, the voice inside my head murmurs again.

"This was never a rescue, Rose. This was a trap."

Something cold twists in my gut.

"We have to leave" I say suddenly.

But the doors slam shut.

The candle flickers out.

And I finally understand.

Julie was not hunting us.

We were walking straight to her.

The candle flickers once—

then dies.

Darkness swallows the room, thick and suffocating, pressing against my skin like the walls of a coffin. My pulse pounds, a frantic rhythm against my ribs. Something is wrong.

A whisper slithers through the silence.

"Welcome home, Rose."

My breath stutters. The voice is neither Julie's nor Jace's. It's Kiva.

A cold, sinking feeling coils in my stomach. My fingers tighten around Rhyse's wrist.

"We need to leave" I say again, my voice sharper now, urgency cutting through my panic.

No one moves.

Lily tilts her head, her expression unreadable in the dim light. "Why?" she asks. "You finally made it back."

"Back?" My voice feels foreign in my throat.

Clover shifts, her dark eyes glinting like a predator waiting for the right moment to pounce. "You really don't remember, do you?"

The air changes.

Not with words. Not with movement. But with something deeper—something unspoken.

The hush in my mind roars to life.

Flashes.

A room bathed in moonlight.

Laughter, but not joy. A knife in the dark.

A name whispered through gritted teeth—Rose. My name. But it wasn't mine first.

My fingers tremble.

"This isn't a rescue" I whisper. "This is a setup."

Dahlia leans forward, her smile slow and deliberate. "You were never just one of us, Rose."

The candlelight suddenly flares back to life, illuminating their faces. But now, they look different.

Not scared. Not fragile.

Calm. Collected. Waiting.

Kiva steps out of the shadows, her lips curling into something cruel.

"Do you understand now?" she murmurs.

A breath shudders from my lungs.

"You were never kidnapped."

The words hit like a gunshot.

"You were one of us" Kiva says, stepping closer, her eyes glinting. "And then you forgot."

No.

No, that's not—

"You ran, Rose. You ran and left us behind."

The walls press in.

I shake my head, but the memories keep coming, not all at once, not clear, but fragmented, sharp, burning.

I see flashes of a different life. A girl in the dark. A promise broken. A betrayal.

My stomach twists violently.

"You knew Julie and Jace long before they took you" Lily murmurs, her voice soft, almost kind. "Because you were with them."

I stagger back, the world tilting.

"You were meant to stay" Kiva says. "You were meant to help us."

The truth slams into me.

I wasn't just another stolen child.

I was a piece of something bigger.

I belonged to them.

And I had tried to escape.

Chapter V

The Past with Thorns

The night is heavy with silence, pressing against my skin like a second layer of flesh. The kind of silence that isn't empty but full, of ghosts, of memories, of things that refuse to stay buried.

Rhyse walks beside me, but neither of us speak. Maybe because words don't fit in the spaces where we stand. Maybe because speaking would make this real.

The world is wider than I remember. The stars blink like forgotten gods, watching, waiting. I feel like I am being seen for the first time, but not by something kind.

"I have always believed if Gods exist they are in hearts, so you can break a temple or a mosque or a church but should not break ones heart. Believing in God gives strength and motivation, similarly, if you think God doesn't want you or seems far away, guess who moved?" I speak to Rhyse but she still stays quiet

Then, a voice cuts through the hush.

"You shouldn't be here."

I freeze.

From the shadows, Magnus steps forward. His face is carved from the same stone as the streets, rough and unreadable, but his eyes, his eyes hold something softer.

Not kindness. Not pity.

Something more dangerous.

Recognition.

"How did you find us?" I ask, my voice a thin thread unraveling in the dark.

Magnus exhales, slow and measured, like he's choosing his words carefully. "I've always known where you were, Rose. You just never knew where to look."

My chest tightens. There is something in his tone, something just beneath the surface, like a wound waiting to be touched.

"Then why didn't you stop them?" Rhyse demands, stepping forward. "If you knew, why didn't you"

"I tried" Magnus interrupts. His voice is quiet, but it cuts. "But some cages are made before you're even born. Some chains are wrapped around your throat before you learn how to breathe."

The weight of his words settles in my bones.

Chains. Cages.

The words drag something out of me. A memory. A wound. A life I forgot.

Flashes.

A small house. A broken window. A woman with tired hands and a man who never looked me in the eyes.

My parents.

They were not cruel, but they were not kind. My mother's love was a fragile thing, something that existed only when it did not inconvenience her. My father spoke in sighs more than in words. They weren't villains, but they weren't saviors either.

I remember the nights I would sit by the door, waiting for them to come home. They never did on time.

I remember the hunger, the cold. The way my mother would brush my hair with gentle hands only after she had been given money by dad who was never on time.

I remember the arguments, the whispers, the way they looked at me when they thought I wasn't watching.

Like I was something temporary.

Like I was something they could trade.

I wasn't the house haunted by ghost, I was a ghost haunted by the house. And I was so lonely that I pretended I was two people so I'd have someone to share with.

I had understood that the planet doesn't need more successful people. The planet desperately needs more peacemakers, healers, restorers, storytellers and kindness of all kinds.

And I always told them

You're asking me what I want to eat, but I am telling you how, when the worst came crashing, my eyes did not spill, my hands did not shake, my breath did not waver.

You're handing me a faded bill from the dry cleaner's down the road, and I am sliding across the table a stack of letters I once wrote to God; pressed with the weight of a six year old's trembling faith, sealed with the kind of fear that keeps you awake at night.

You pour milk into your coffee, a quiet storm of white in the dark, and I am half-laughing about the psychiatrist's office, how there is actually a couch, how it is blue tweed, how it feels like a waiting room for lost souls.

You are trying to do the ordinary things. I am tearing open old wounds and placing them between my fingers like salt on the table. I do not know how to be silent anymore.

These are the things I have done, and they sit heavy in my chest. These are the places I have been, and they left bruises on my soul. Life has stitched itself into the curve of my spine, each vertebra aching beneath its weight.

And yet; here we are. You, stirring sugar into the silence. Me, unraveling thread by thread. The morning stretches on, long and indifferent, carrying three of us toward something neither of us can name.

I told my mother, I'll memorize the melody of your favorite song, let it echo through my mind until the words carve themselves into every hollow space within me. But I'll forget the small things; the way your hands linger around a coffee cup, why you never reach for tea, the way your voice sounds in the quiet before dawn. I will remember how your laughter filled a room, but forget the way it slowly faded when you looked at me.

Loving me is like chasing shadows; no matter how close you get, there will always be parts of me you cannot touch. And when you finally see that, I will write you into the margins of every page until my fingers ache, until my ribs feel like collapsing walls, until every syllable is a wound that refuses to close. I will turn you into poetry, into metaphors I whisper to the stars, into verses that sound like apologies but never quite are.

But now I feel, I should have held onto the warmth of your touch instead of counting the constellations of freckles on your skin. I should have memorized the way you smiled at sunrise rather than the way your footsteps faded at dusk. I should have paid more attention to the softness of your voice when you said my name, instead of the silence that followed when you no longer did. I should have given you something worth staying for, something softer than regret, something warmer than an empty cup; something more than words written too late.

A least gift a father can give to their child is to keep their mother happy, and no matter how far it went I always believed positive.

"Your parents weren't innocent, Rose" Magnus says, pulling me back to the present. "They made a choice. And it wasn't to keep you."

The words slice through me, leaving behind something raw and bleeding.

"They sold me" I whisper.

Magnus doesn't flinch. "They gave you away before you could even ask why."

A bitter laugh bubbles up from my throat. "And you're telling me Julie and Jace were the better option?"

"No" Magnus murmurs. "I'm telling you there were never good options."

Silence wraps around us again. But this silence is different. This silence is truth.

For years, I told myself I was stolen from a life that missed me. That somewhere, a mother cried for her lost child, a father searched the streets for the daughter he never got to protect.

But that was a story I told myself so I wouldn't break.

The truth is simpler. Colder.

They let me go.

They let me become someone else's problem.

I don't know how long I stand there, drowning in the weight of it. The night is quiet except for the hum of the streetlights, the whisper of the wind.

Magnus sighs. "The past is a garden that will never bloom again, Rose. You can keep watering it with your tears, but all you'll ever grow is grief."

His words settle somewhere deep inside me, planting themselves like seeds in the hollow spaces of my ribs.

I do not respond.

Because I do not know what kind of flower will bloom from this pain.

But I know one thing.

I will not wither here.

The streetlights flicker, buzzing like dying fireflies in the heavy dark. My breath is slow, measured, but my thoughts are wild, clawing, tearing, desperate to piece together a past that no longer belongs to me.

Magnus watches me, his face unreadable, his eyes carrying the weight of something unspoken. I wonder how much he knows, how much he has always known.

"You never told me" I say, my voice sharper than I intend. "You never told me the truth about them."

"Would it have changed anything?" Magnus replies, tilting his head slightly. "Would you have run faster? Hated less? Broken sooner?"

I hate how easily he reads me.

Rhyse is silent beside me, but I can feel her presence; a quiet, steady force, grounding me in a world that is suddenly shifting beneath my feet.

I inhale. Exhale. My ribs ache with the weight of my own breath.

Memories bleed back in.

I was six when I realized my parents were not heroes.

They fought in whispers, their words laced with things I didn't understand.

Debt. Money. Choices. Consequences.

My father carried his regret in his fists, though he never used them on me. He used them on the walls, the table, the steering wheel of his old car that always smelled like rust and stale smoke.

My mother carried hers in her silence, in the way she looked at me without really looking at me; like I was an inconvenience she had grown too tired to acknowledge.

But some nights, when the air was still and the world outside our window had settled into its quiet slumber, she would sit beside me and run her fingers through my hair.

"Sleep, my little flower" she would whisper. "Tomorrow will be better."

But tomorrow was never better.

It was cold breakfasts and locked doors. It was hushed conversations with people who never stayed long. It was an empty fridge and an emptier home.

And then, one day, it was nothing at all.

Because one day, I woke up and they were gone.

One day, I woke up and Julie was there instead.

My throat is dry when I speak again the same question "They didn't sell me, did they?"

Magnus doesn't move. "Oh come on Rose, Not in the way you're thinking."

I let out a hollow laugh. "Then how?"

His silence is my answer.

And that's when I realize, he won't say it because I already know.

My parents didn't wake up one morning and decide to sell their daughter like a piece of furniture. No, it happened slowly. It happened in the way debts piled up like dead leaves, in the way desperation ate at them like rot in the foundation of a home.

They didn't sell me.

They surrendered me.

And somehow, that feels worse.

The stars above seem farther away now, the sky stretching endlessly, endlessly, endlessly, like a question that will never have an answer.

Magnus shifts, and for the first time, his voice is softer. "Hate them if you must, Rose. But don't waste your life waiting for ghosts to apologize."

I close my eyes. The ghosts are already here.

I carry them in my spine, in the marrow of my bones. I carry them in the spaces between my ribs, where their absence has built a home.

I carry them in my name. The name they did not care enough to keep.

Magnus sighs again. "I told you, The past is a garden that will never bloom again, Rose. You can keep watering it with your tears, but all you'll ever grow is grief."

I stare at him, at the deep lines on his face, at the weariness that clings to his frame like an old coat. And catch every meaning in what he spoke once again.

"And what if I don't want to grow at all?" I ask.

Magnus gives me a sad smile. "Then you'll be exactly what they wanted you to be."

The words strike something deep inside me, something sharp and aching, but before I can respond, Rhyse steps closer.

"We can't stay here," she says. "They'll come back. They always come back."

She's right.

Julie, Jace, Kiva— they are not finished.

They let us think we were free. They let us believe, for a moment, that we had escaped.

But we were never running away.

We were just being let go.

Like flowers plucked too soon, left to wither in the dark.

I look back at Magnus. His expression is unreadable again, his hands deep in his coat pockets, his gaze somewhere between past and present.

"What do we do now?" I ask.

Magnus exhales. "You decide. You can chase a past that will never change, or you can choose to live."

The wind shifts. The city hums. The night waits.

And for the first time in a long, long time—

I don't know what I want.

The night stretches endlessly, its silence thick like smoke curling through the streets. The weight of Magnus words still clings to my skin, heavy as old dust in forgotten rooms.

"Your parents made a choice. And it wasn't to keep you." Echos.

I do not cry. Not because I do not want to, but because I do not know how.

I have spent years grieving ghosts, mourning a mother and father who never mourned me. But how do you grieve something that was never truly yours?

Magnus walks beside me, his presence like an old book, worn, knowing, filled with stories I am not yet ready to read. Rhyse trails behind, quiet as always, her silence no longer just a habit, but a wound too deep to stitch.

"Where do we go now?" I ask.

Magnus exhales, his breath curling in the cold air. "Wherever the past doesn't follow."

I almost laugh. The past never let go. It clings to your ribs, whispers in your ear, waits in the dark corners of your mind. It is not a road that can be walked away from; it is the ground beneath your feet.

"You don't understand," I say. "I still hear them."

"Your parents?" Magnus asks, but he already knows the answer.

I nod, pressing my fingers to my temples, as if I can smother the voices that still haunt me. Their absence speaks louder than their presence ever did.

Flashes.

My mother, sitting at the kitchen table, an apple in one hand, a bill in the other

"Not today, Rose. I don't have the time."

My father, slouched on the couch, the television humming in the background. A man who spoke in sighs, in unfinished sentences, in apologies that never quite reached his lips.

"Go to your room."

I was a child who learned young that love was not always warm, that some hands are made for holding but others for letting go.

The house was small, the walls thin, the arguments thick. I did not know hunger the way I know it now, but I knew what it meant to want something you could never have.

A mother's full attention.

A father's steady hands.

A home that did not feel like a waiting room.

"You think love is supposed to be grand" Magnus says, pulling me from the memory. "But love is simple. It is presence. It is choosing someone even when the world says you don't have to."

I swallow hard. "Then they never loved me."

Magnus stops walking. The streetlamp casts a hollow glow over his face, deepening the lines carved into his skin. "Maybe they did" he says. "But they loved their survival more."

The words slice through me, bitter and true.

Survival. That is what it had always been. A game of who could make it through the day.

They did not have time to love me. They were too busy trying to love themselves.

I wonder if they ever succeeded.

I wonder if they even tried.

The city hums in the distance, a living thing, pulsing, breathing, waiting.

Magnus turns to me, his voice softer now. "You have two choices, Rose. You can keep chasing a childhood that is already buried. Or you can plant something new."

"Like what?" I ask.

He looks at me for a long moment. Then, he simply says:

"A life."

I do not respond.

Because I do not know what life is supposed to feel like.

All I have ever known is survival.

And survival is not living.

It is simply not dying.

The wind shifts, carrying the scent of distant rain. I exhale, watching my breath turn to mist, a fleeting ghost disappearing into the night.

Magnus words linger in my ribs. You can plant something new.

But I have never known how to plant. I have only known how to be uprooted.

I glance at Rhyse. She has been quiet, more than usual. Her eyes are fixed ahead, lost in some place my voice cannot reach.

"What about you?" I ask. "What will you plant?"

She doesn't answer.

Maybe because she, too, doesn't know what life is supposed to feel like. Maybe because she, too, has only ever known how to survive.

Maybe because she never expected to make it this far.

We stop beneath an old bridge, where the streetlights flicker like dying stars. The city hums beyond us, unaware of the two ghosts standing in its shadows.

Magnus reaches into his coat and pulls out something small. A photograph.

He hands it to me.

I stare at it.

It is worn, edges curling, the ink slightly faded. But the image is still clear.

A girl. Me.

No older than six, standing in a dimly lit kitchen. My hair is uncombed, my clothes slightly too big. A birthday cake sits in front of me; small, uneven, the candle already half-melted.

Behind me, my mother leans against the counter, she is looking at me, but not with a smile. Not with warmth.

With indifference.

And next to her—

Jace.

My breath catches.

"What-- "

"He wasn't just your captor" Magnus says quietly. "He was there before."

The ground tilts. The air turns sharp.

"He knew your parents?" My voice is barely a whisper.

Magnus nods. "He wasn't always Julie's. He was theirs first."

I look back at the photograph. Jace is younger here, but his eyes are the same; calculating, unreadable. He is leaning against the kitchen wall, arms crossed, watching the scene like an outsider, like a man who doesn't belong but refuses to leave.

"He was part of their world before he took you" Magnus continues. "Before he and Julie ran."

My fingers tighten around the photograph.

"Ran?"

"They weren't just kidnappers" Magnus says. "They were deserters."

A hollow feeling settles in my stomach.

This is not just about me. This is not just about my parents selling me.

This is about what they were selling me into.

The hush inside me roars.

Memories stir, half-formed, fractured, refusing to fit together. The cold kitchen tiles beneath my feet. The smoke curling through the air. The hushed whispers behind closed doors.

Jace was there.

Watching. Waiting.

But waiting for what?

My hands tremble. The photograph feels heavier now, as if it holds more than just ink and paper.

It holds secrets.

It holds answers I might not want.

I look up at Magnus. "Why are you telling me this now?"

"Because the past isn't done with you, Rose" he says. "And whether you chase it or not, it's already chasing you."

My stomach twists.

Julie, Jace, Kiva.

They didn't disappear into nothing. They didn't run because they were afraid.

They ran because they were returning to something.

Something bigger than them.

Something that was always meant to find me.

I shove the photograph into my pocket, my pulse a wild, uneven thing.

"Then let it come" I murmur.

Magnus watches me carefully. "Are you ready for that?"

I don't know.

But I do know one thing.

I have spent eleven years being hunted.

It's time I start hunting back.

The night is quiet, but it is not peaceful. It is the kind of quiet that comes before a storm, before a scream, before something shatters beyond repair.

And something is shattering.

Me.

The weight of Magnus's words still lingers, but now it is nothing compared to the weight of what I am seeing. What I am understanding.

Rhyse.

Her hands are tucked into the sleeves of her sweater, her lips pressed together, her breath steady. Too steady.

Like she is bracing for something.

Like she has already seen this moment play out.

"Say something" I murmur. "Anything."

She exhales. "There's nothing to say."

Lies.

There is everything to say.

The hush in my mind returns, slithering through my veins, whispering truths I was never meant to find. Not yet.

Julie's voice echoes in my head, distant but sharp. "She's quiet. She listens. She learns."

Jace's hand on my shoulder. "You'll understand when you're older."

Kiva's smirk. "You really thought this was the end?"

And Rhyse— always there. Always watching.

Watching me.

The realization creeps in, slow and poisonous.

"You knew" I whisper.

Rhyse stiffens, but she doesn't answer.

"You knew what they were doing" I say, my voice shaking. "Before they ever took me."

Something flickers across her face—not shock. Not confusion.

Acceptance.

Like she has been waiting for this.

The world tips beneath my feet.

"You were part of it" I breathe.

Rhyse finally meets my gaze, and I see it.

Not fear. Not regret.

Recognition.

"I was never locked in that cellar, Rose" she murmurs.

My stomach twists. My pulse roars in my ears.

She steps closer, her voice quiet but sharp enough to cut.

"I stayed because I wanted to."

The words knock the air from my lungs.

No.

No, that's not—

That's not the truth.

But it is.

It always was.

Rhyse never fought to leave.

Rhyse never screamed.

Rhyse never tried.

Because she didn't have to.

Because she wasn't a prisoner.

She was a witness.

She was one of them.

The ground beneath me isn't real. The air around me isn't real. Nothing feels real.

But Rhyse is.

She stands there, unshaken, unafraid, like she has been waiting for me to catch up.

"You're lying" I whisper, but the words taste hollow. "You were just a kid. They took you, just like they took me."

Rhyse tilts her head slightly. Almost pitying.

"Did they?"

The hush inside me howls.

Flashes.

Julie's hands, gentle in my hair. "You'll understand one day, Rose."

Jace watching me from the doorway, the way someone watches their own creation.

Kiva's voice, sharp as a blade. "Some flowers grow wild. Others are planted."

Rhyse, always silent, always waiting. But never suffering.

Never starving like I did.

Never crying like I did.

Never breaking like I did.

Because she wasn't meant to.

Because she wasn't stolen.

Because she chose this.

"Why?" My voice barely escapes my throat. "Why would you stay?"

Rhyse exhales, slow and measured. "Because I believed in them."

The words feel like ice against my skin.

Magnus shifts beside me, his expression darkening. "Believed in what, exactly?"

Rhyse finally smiles. But it isn't joy. It isn't relief.

It is understanding.

"You were never the only one, Rose" she says softly. "You were just the only one who forgot."

The streetlights hum. The city breathes. My pulse pounds like a drum.

"I tried to remind you" she continues. "But you weren't ready to remember."

I step back.

"I was a prisoner" I snap.

Rhyse shakes her head.

"No, Rose." Her voice is quiet, but the weight of it crushes me.

The hush inside me screams.

The city watches us, but it does not care. The stars blink, but they do not see. The night listens, but it does not whisper back.

I am alone with the weight of her words.

"You were being prepared."

Prepared for what?

Prepared for who?

I want to scream. I want to shake her until she cracks, until she bleeds, until she tells me that it's all a lie. That she suffered like I did. That she was stolen, not chosen.

But she just stands there, quiet, still, waiting.

I feel sick.

The wind is cold, but I am burning. My mind claws at the walls of my skull, desperate to make sense of something that refuses to be understood.

"What did they want from me?" I ask. My voice is thin, fraying at the edges. "What was I supposed to become?"

Rhyse looks at me, and for the first time tonight, something flickers across her face.

Pity.

"They never told me" she admits. "I only knew my part. I was supposed to stay close to you. Keep you from running. Make sure you became what they needed."

I want to laugh. I want to tear the world apart.

"So what now?" I say bitterly. "What happens now that I know?"

Rhyse shrugs. "That's up to them."

The words slam into me like a bullet.

"Them."

Julie. Jace. Kiva.

The past that refuses to die. The ghosts that refuse to stay buried. The hands that shaped me into something I do not understand.

I press my fingers to my temples, digging into my skin like I can tear the thoughts out of my skull. My lungs feel too small, my ribs too tight, the sky too far.

"I don't know what to do" I whisper.

Magnus watches me, his face carved from stone. "Then do nothing" he says simply.

I look at him, startled. "What?"

"You don't always have to know, Rose" Magnus murmurs. "The world will break you either way. The only difference is whether you shatter on your own terms."

I swallow hard. His words should bring comfort, but they don't. They feel like an obituary written before I've even died.

"We should rest" Rhyse says suddenly.

Rest.

As if sleep will change what I have learned.

As if dreams will rewrite the past.

But my body is tired. My mind is exhausted.

Without another word, we walk.

We find an empty, abandoned apartment. The kind no one cares about, the kind that belongs to no one. The kind that swallows lost things whole.

Magnus settles into the corner, arms crossed, eyes closing but never truly resting.

Rhyse curls up near the window, staring at the sky, lost in thoughts I no longer trust.

And me?

I lie down, staring at the ceiling, the cracks forming patterns I do not understand.

My mind is loud. Too loud.

"The world is cruel."

"The world is unreal."

"Nothing makes sense."

"Nothing feels real."

"I don't know what's happening."

"I don't know what's coming."

"I don't know who I am."

"I was better in the cellar."

"At least I knew what sadness was there."

"At least I didn't have to question it."

"I think I have always been sad."

"And maybe, I always will be."

The night breathes, slow and heavy, pressing down on my ribs like a weight I cannot lift. My body aches, but not in the way hunger aches. This pain has no source, no cure, no name.

I blink, and the tears slip free before I can stop them. Warm, silent, betraying.

They trail down my face, sinking into the cold floor beneath me, as if the earth itself is drinking my grief, as if the ground has been starved of sorrow and I am its only offering.

I do not sob. Sobs are loud. Sobs demand to be heard.

But I have learned that silence is softer. Silence is easier to hide.

The world outside is endless, yet I feel trapped within it.

I do not know what I am running from, nor what I am running toward.

Perhaps there is no difference.

<u>Perhaps the world itself is just another kind of cellar; wider, louder, but just as hollow.</u>

At least when I was locked away, I did not have to wonder.

At least when I was starving, I did not have to question if I was meant to be fed.

I was safer when I was suffering.

At least then, I knew what pain was.

At least then, I did not have to call it something else.

A shuddering breath. A quiet surrender.

I close my eyes.

The darkness greets me like an old friend, and I let it hold me.

I sleep.

Chapter VI

Confronting The Past

The next morning we wake up, the morning sun scatters against the broken glass windows, whispering secrets to those who listen.

But we are not listening.

We are waiting.

Magnus brings milk with cereals, we all drink and eat some biscuits.

The air is thick, wrapped in something unseen, something heavy. The kind of silence that doesn't come from peace but from the weight of stories left untold. I feel it pressing against my ribs, curling around my throat like vines that do not strangle, but do not let go.

Magnus keeps the dishes and leans against the far wall, arms crossed, his shadow stretching long in the dim candlelight. Rhyse sits near the window, her expression unreadable, as if she's listening to something none of us can hear. And across from us, they sit.

Lily. Clover. Dahlia. Daisy.

Names that should have belonged to something soft, something bright.

But their eyes do not bloom.

Their hands do not tremble like petals in the wind.

They are not flowers.

Not anymore.

They were supposed to be gardens.

Instead, they were turned to stone.

Lily speaks first.

Her voice is quiet, the kind that drifts through the air like forgotten music. Her hair falls in dark curls over her shoulder, wild, unkempt, as if it refuses to be tamed. There is something steady in her gaze, something that does not ask for permission.

"We've been waiting for you" she says. Not as a greeting. Not as a welcome. As a fact.

I swallow. "For me?"

Clover tilts her head, eyes sharp as broken glass. Her features are delicate, almost ethereal, but her presence is something else

Entirely something unmovable, something that does not bow to storms. "You were always meant to return."

I glance at Rhyse, but she doesn't look at me.

"I don't understand," I say, the words hollow in my mouth. "Who are you?"

Dahlia lets out a slow, bitter laugh. She is taller than the others, her frame lean, her eyes carrying a weight that should not belong to someone so young. "We are what you left behind."

The hush in my mind twists.

Daisy speaks last. She is the smallest of them, but there is no weakness in her. Her voice is smooth, her posture composed. "We are what you were supposed to become."

A cold shiver slides down my spine.

"You don't remember us, do you?" Lily asks, tilting her head slightly, studying me as if searching for the pieces I lost.

"I don't—" My voice catches. "I don't know what I was supposed to remember."

Dahlia leans forward, resting her elbows on her knees. "Then let me remind you."

Flashes.

A dimly lit room. The scent of earth and something metallic in the air.

Laughter, not joyful, but sharp, edged with something darker.

Hands gripping my wrists, not in violence, but in training.

"You have to be stronger, Rose."

Julie's voice.

"You have to be willing to do what needs to be done."

The voices.

Not just Julie. Not just Jace. Not just Kiva.

Lily.

Clover.

Dahlia.

Daisy.

They were there.

Not caged.

Not stolen.

Chosen.

--

A breath shudders out of me as I return to the present. The candle flickers. The room is too quiet. The walls feel too close.

"You were one of us," Clover says simply.

The words sink deep, carving themselves into my ribs.

"I ran," I whisper.

"You did," Dahlia confirms. "And we never understood why."

I clench my hands into fists, nails pressing into my palms. "Because this, whatever this was, it wasn't right."

Lily exhales, a ghost of something resembling sadness in her eyes. "Right and wrong don't exist when survival is the only rule."

"We were flowers, Rose." Daisy murmurs. "But we were raised as stone."

Something inside me cracks.

I look at Magnus. He hasn't spoken, hasn't moved. His face is unreadable, but there is something in his eyes, something heavy.

"You knew," I accuse.

Magnus doesn't deny it. "I knew pieces. But the truth is never whole until you see it yourself."

My stomach twists.

Julie, Jace, Kiva—whatever they were shaping me into, it was never just me.

It was us.

All of us.

But for what?

Rhyse finally speaks. Her voice is quieter than I have ever heard it.

"They wanted us to be their weapons."

The words feel like ice in my veins.

"They called us flowers," she continues, "but flowers are fragile. Flowers wilt." She lifts her gaze, and for the first time, I see it the years of silence, the weight of knowing, the burden of never speaking.

"So they made us something else."

Lily nods. "We were raised to be unbreakable."

Clover smirks, but it doesn't reach her eyes. "We were meant to be beautiful, but deadly."

Dahlia stretches out her hand, fingers curling slightly, as if holding something unseen. "They taught us how to blend in. How to be overlooked. How to move unseen."

Daisy's voice is softer. "But most of all, they taught us how to obey."

I shake my head. "I don't—I didn't—"

"You left before they could finish with you" Lily says. "But we didn't."

I feel sick.

"Then why did you stay?" My voice is hoarse, almost desperate. "Why didn't you run?"

Dahlia's lips curl into something close to a smile, but there is no joy in it. "Where would we have gone?"

The hush inside me is screaming now.

Julie. Jace. Kiva.

They didn't steal children.

They built them.

Built us.

I stand abruptly, the chair scraping against the floor. The air is too thick, the walls too close, my skin too tight.

"I can't—" I shake my head. "I can't do this."

"Then don't," Magnus says simply.

I whip around to face him. "That's all you have to say?"

Magnus meets my gaze, and there is something ancient in his expression. "What do you want me to say, Rose?"

"I want you to tell me what the hell I'm supposed to do now!" I snap. "I want you to tell me why this happened, why I was a part of this, why I can't remember all of it, why—"

I stop.

Because Magnus is watching me the way people watch a wildfire.

Not with fear.

Not with pity.

With understanding.

Because he's seen this before.

Because he knows what comes next.

And that terrifies me more than anything else.

The room is silent.

The candle burns low.

The night presses against the windows, listening.

And then, Magnus speaks.

"This was never about what they made you," he says quietly. "It's about what you choose to be now."

His words settle in my bones, wrapping around the hollowness inside me.

I glance at Rhyse. Her expression is unreadable, but there is something in her eyes—something fragile, something waiting.

I look at Lily, Clover, Dahlia, and Daisy.

They are flowers in name only.

Their roots were cut.

Their petals were torn.

Their beauty was sharpened into something that doesn't wither.

And now, I must decide—

Am I still a flower?

Or have I turned to stone, too?

But am I a weak stone

The leaves outside breathes.

The city hums.

The answer waits.

The air is heavier now. It clings to my skin like the weight of a thousand unseen hands. The candle flickers, the flames licking at the darkness, but it does not chase away the cold seeping into my bones.

Rhyse's confession still lingers in the air, a ghost that refuses to leave. She was never a prisoner. Never a victim. She was planted, just like the others. Just like me.

I look at them—Lily, Clover, Dahlia, Daisy.

Flowers in name, but shaped into something unbending. They were meant to be gardens, but they were raised in stone.

And then Daisy speaks again.

"I never believed you were truly gone," she says. "Not really."

There is something strange in her voice, something that doesn't quite fit with the rest. Her gaze is softer, her words careful, measured, like she's walking on the edges of something fragile.

"I used to dream about you," she continues, and something in my chest tightens. "Even when they told me you were never coming back, I knew."

I frown. "Knew what?"

Daisy hesitates. For the first time, she looks unsure.

And then, Magnus speaks.

"She knew because she was looking for you."

The words stop my breath. The hush inside me coils like a serpent waiting to strike.

"What?" I whisper.

Magnus doesn't look at me. He looks at Daisy.

"Tell her" he says.

Daisy's fingers tighten into fists.

"Rose…" Her voice is almost too soft to hear. "I think I'm your sister."

The candlelight flickers, stretching shadows across the walls. I shake my head, but the pieces in my mind are already shifting, falling into place, clicking together in ways I never expected.

"No," I breathe. "That's not—"

But my voice dies. Because suddenly, I see it.

The familiarity. The way Daisy's voice always felt like a whisper from a life I couldn't remember. The way her presence made something deep inside me ache, something beyond the trauma, beyond the past I thought I knew.

The way her face—

No.

I don't remember her. But my body does.

"Tell me you're lying," I say. My voice shakes, but I don't care. "Tell me this is some kind of mistake."

Daisy swallows hard. "I wish I could."

The room is spinning. I press my fingers against my face, trying to breathe.

"You don't remember because they took you first," she continues. "You were only seven. I was barely five."

I stagger back, my mind screaming against the truth clawing its way in.

Seven.

Five.

The timeline fits.

"They told me you ran away," Daisy murmurs. "They told me you didn't want to come back."

Her voice breaks.

"But I never stopped looking for you."

I stare at her, my breath shallow, my ribs tightening around the weight of everything I thought I knew.

"You're my sister." The words taste foreign in my mouth, like they don't belong to me.

Daisy gives a small, broken nod. "I think so."

The hush inside me does not whisper. It screams.

The past was never just something I lost.

It was something they stole.

And now, it's coming back to haunt us all.

The words still echo in my ribs, pressing against my lungs like a weight I cannot shake.

Daisy is my sister.

I don't know how to accept that.

I don't know if I want to.

But the world doesn't wait for me to understand.

The candle has burned low, its flame weak, barely clinging to life. The air is thick with something unsaid, something bigger than any of us.

"We need to go," Rhyse says finally. Her voice is quiet but firm, unshaken. "We need to find them."

Julie. Jace. Kiva.

The ones who made us.

The ones who broke us.

The ones who still hold the answers we don't have.

I swallow hard. "And if they don't want to be found?"

Lily smirks, but there is no humor in it. "Then we'll make them wish they never hid."

Her words should bring me comfort. They don't.

Magnus shifts against the wall, his gaze unreadable. "This isn't going to end the way you think," he warns. "You're chasing ghosts. And ghosts don't give answers."

Dahlia tilts her head. "Maybe not. But they leave footprints."

And that's enough for us to follow.

She stands in the dark, not a reflection, not a memory; a girl who was left behind. A version of me that should not exist. Her skin is pale, stretched tight over bones that have known nothing but waiting. Her eyes—my eyes—are hollow, filled with something I do not understand.

Something that has seen everything I have forgotten.

Something that has been waiting for me to return.

And behind her—

Rhyse.

She stands just beyond the threshold, not moving, not speaking, but not stopping this either.

Because she already knew.

Because she has always known.

I turn to her, and for the first time, she looks away first.

"You knew," I whisper, voice raw. "You always knew."

The others do not move. They do not interrupt.

Rhyse exhales, slow, quiet, like she is carrying something too heavy to hold, something she should have let fall years ago. But she didn't.

She held it. She held me.

"I tried," she says finally. "I tried to let you forget."

Let.

Not force. Not trick. Let.

And that is what breaks me most.

Not that she was on their side. Not that she stayed when I ran.

But that she let me believe she was suffering with me.

That she let me grieve with her. Let me whisper to her in the dark, let me believe that we were trapped together, let me hold her hand as if we were the same.

And all this time—

She was grieving me.

She was holding the hand of a girl who was already gone.

"You were supposed to stay," she murmurs, and it is not an accusation. It is a confession.

"You were supposed to stay, and I was supposed to keep you here."

The words sink, slow, heavy. Not a lie. A truth she was never meant to say.

"You were supposed to be part of them," I say, voice shaking, "not me."

She exhales. Does not deny it.

"I wasn't given a flower name because I wasn't supposed to be like you," she says. "I was never supposed to be one of you."

I was.

I was the one who was supposed to bloom.

And yet, I was the one who wilted.

I stare at her, the only person I have ever trusted, the only person I thought I understood.

And I wonder—

Has she been mourning me all this time?

Has she been standing in the wreckage of what I should have been, watching as I turned into something I was never meant to be?

Was she trying to protect me?

Or was she trying to bring me back?

Is she still?

The girl in the dark—*the version of me that was left behind—*shifts, stepping forward.

But I do not look at her.

I look at Rhyse.

Because for the first time, she does not look like a villain.

She does not look like a traitor.

She looks like a girl who has been drowning in her own silence.

She looks like someone who never got to choose who she became.

And suddenly, I do not want revenge.

I do not want justice.

I do not want to hurt her the way she has hurt me.

I just want to understand.

I step forward. Rhyse does not move.

"Tell me," I whisper. "Tell me why."

And for the first time, she does.

Rhyse breathes in, slow, quiet, as if she is inhaling all the years we lost, as if she is pulling the weight of it into her lungs before it breaks her ribs apart. She has carried something for too long. And now—now she has no choice but to put it down.

She looks at me, and for the first time, she does not wear silence like armor.

"Because I thought I could save you," she says.

A pause. A crack in the air. A wound splitting open.

"I thought if I kept you from remembering, then maybe you wouldn't have to become what they wanted."

Her voice is raw, stripped of its usual emptiness. It is the sound of something breaking.

I stare at her, pulse slow, heartbeat thick with something I do not understand.

"You let them erase me," I say, but it is not an accusation. It is an understanding.

Her hands clench. "Yes."

A slow exhale. A confession we can never take back.

"I let them take you so they wouldn't take all of you."

I do not blink.

I let her words settle into my skin like a wound that will never scab over.

Rhyse turns slightly, gaze drifting to the others. Daisy, Dahlia, Clover, Lily.

"They gave you names of flowers," she murmurs, almost to herself. "Because they wanted you to be something beautiful before they crushed you."

The words feel like thorns against my ribs.

"And you?" I ask, voice thin, fragile. "Why weren't you given one?"

She exhales, slow. "Because I was never meant to be picked. I was the soil beneath you, the ground they planted you in. I was supposed to stay where I was, to hold you in place."

Her voice does not waver. But her hands shake.

I should hate her. But I don't.

Because I understand now.

She was never meant to bloom.

She was meant to wither alongside us, keeping us from running, keeping us from breaking, keeping us from realizing that we were already dying.

A garden full of stolen things, tended by hands that never knew how to love without control.

I inhale sharply. "And you believed them?"

A long pause.

"No."

She meets my gaze, and there is something in her eyes that is breaking, something that has been waiting to shatter.

"I believed in you."

And that—that is what destroys me the most.

Rhyse was never one of us, but she was never one of them either.

She existed between the cracks, in the spaces where light did not touch, in the silence between screams.

She let me go, but she did not follow.

She let me forget, but she did not stop remembering.

And now—now she stands before me, empty-handed, holding nothing but the weight of everything she has done, everything she has lost, everything she was never allowed to want.

I step forward.

For the first time in years, she steps back.

Not out of fear.

But because she does not know if she deserves to stand beside me anymore.

The air is heavy. The past is heavier.

But I reach for her wrist anyway.

I do not forgive her.

But I do not let her stand alone.

Because maybe—maybe we were never meant to bloom.

Maybe we were just meant to survive.

Rhyse's breath is shallow, her silence no longer armor but an open wound. I see it now—the years she spent trapped between two worlds, the girl who never belonged to herself, the sister who was never my sister at all.

But before I can speak, before I can decide whether to hold her closer or push her away, the door behind us creaks open.

A shadow spills into the dim light.

Someone steps forward..

A man and a woman. Older. Tired. Unfamiliar.

No—not unfamiliar.

A memory buried so deep I forgot I ever carried it.

My parents.

My real parents.

For a moment, I do not breathe.

The woman stares at me, her lips trembling, her hands clutching the edges of her coat as if she is holding onto something fragile. The man beside her is stiff, his face unreadable.

But his eyes—his eyes are the same as mine.

A lifetime of silence stretches between us, thick and suffocating. And then—

The woman—my mother?—steps forward.

"Rose" she breathes. Like she has been waiting a lifetime to say my name.

Something inside me cracks.

She lifts a shaking hand, as if she wants to touch me, to hold me, to make up for years she cannot give back.

But she stops herself.

And then—the apology.

"We are so sorry" she whispers.

I feel Daisy shift beside me. Dahlia is staring, lips parted slightly. Magnus watches without blinking.

Rhyse is silent.

I should feel something. I should feel everything. But all I feel is—

Confusion.

I glance at Julie. At Jace. At Kiva.

The ones who told me my parents never searched for me. That they sold me. That I was unwanted.

They say nothing.

Because they know.

They have been caught.

And then—the truth.

"You weren't sold," my father says. His voice is rough, frayed at the edges, worn with guilt. "You were stolen."

The room does not breathe.

I hear nothing but the hush inside me—but this time, it is not whispering.

It is listening.

"For what?" I ask, my voice strange to my own ears.

My mother hesitates, then says the words that rip the world apart.

"For your blood."

Silence.

Blood?

My pulse is slow, thick, dragging.

I turn to Julie, Jace, Kiva. The architects of my suffering.

Jace exhales through his nose. "Well. That's unfortunate."

Julie tilts her head, a smirk playing at the edges of her mouth. Not regret. Not fear. Amusement.

Kiva shrugs. "Should've let her forget."

My blood.

I do not know what it means.

I do not know why.

But I know one thing—this was never about me.

It was about what I was made of.

Julie sighs. "Well, we had a good run, didn't we?" She turns to Jace. "We should kill them now, right?"

Jace rubs his jaw, considering. "We could. Or we could run. Again."

"I vote kill" Kiva offers.

Magnus steps forward. "I vote you shut up."

Dahlia pulls out a knife. "I vote stabbing."

Daisy raises a hand. "I vote running and screaming."

Lily sighs. "Daisy, stop voting."

Clover deadpans, "I vote we start voting seriously."

Julie rolls her eyes. "Oh, for God's sake."

And then—chaos.

Julie moves first, fast, sharp, grabbing for the gun at her waist; but Magnus is faster. He slams into her, sending them both crashing into the wall.

Jace reaches for my mother. I do not let him.

I lunge, colliding into him, knocking him backward. His grip is strong, too strong, but I am not seven anymore.

I am not a little girl waiting to be saved.

I am my own storm.

Rhyse moves, grabbing for my arm—but this time, I pull her instead.

She hesitates.

For a second, just a second.

And that is all I need.

I throw her back, stepping between her and the others, and for the first time—she does not fight me.

For the first time, she lets me go.

Kiva disappears into the dark. Coward.

Julie is screaming. Jace is cursing.

Dahlia is stabbing someone.

Daisy is screaming.

Lily is dragging Magnus toward the door.

I do not stop moving.

I do not look back.

Because if I do—I will see Rhyse.

And if I see her, I will break.

I will wither.

We reach the outside, lungs full of cold, heavy air.

The house behind us groans, the weight of its ghosts pressing against its walls.

My mother grabs my wrist.

"We have to go," she gasps.

I pull back.

My father's voice is desperate. "Rose, please."

And suddenly, I laugh.

Not because it is funny. But because it is tragic.

Because this is not a family reunion.

This is a war.

And I do not know who I am fighting for anymore.

I wipe my mouth, tasting blood, tasting freedom, tasting something that does not belong to me.

I look at them—the parents who lost me.

I look at Rhyse—the sister who was never mine.

And I say—

"I'm not going anywhere."

Not until this ends.

Not until they pay.

The hush inside me is silent.

Because for the first time—

It is waiting for me to decide.

Chapter X

The Weight of Blood
The Lie of Love

Blood pools beneath my feet, thick, black under the moonlight. My breath is shallow, my ribs caged with something I cannot name. The night stretches infinitely, but the truth is closing in. My parents—the ones who lost me, the ones who left me, the ones who stand before me now with hollow apologies and trembling hands—say my name like it is something sacred. Like it is something stolen. Like it is something that was never truly mine.

I want to laugh. I want to scream. I want to rip my own name from my skin and ask them if it ever belonged to me at all.

Julie is watching, eyes glinting in the dim light, lips curling in something like amusement, something like pity. Jace does not move, but his hand is still near his weapon, still waiting. Kiva is somewhere in the dark, watching from the shadows like she always does, like a whisper never meant to be heard.

And Rhyse—Rhyse has not spoken.

Because Rhyse already knows the truth.

She has always known.

My mother takes a step forward. "Rose," she breathes, but it is not a plea. It is not relief. It is grief.

Because she knows, too.

She knows that I do not belong to her anymore.

And maybe I never did.

I tilt my head. I ask, because I have to, because my soul is unraveling, because the hush inside me is screaming.

"Why?"

Why did you leave me? Why did you let them take me? Why did you never come back? Why are you here now, after all these years, after all these deaths, after all this suffering?

Why was I stolen?

Julie smiles. She is enjoying this. She is a wolf that has already devoured the lamb, a god amused by the suffering of the mortals beneath her. She tilts her head toward my mother. "Go on, then. Tell her."

My mother's hands shake.

My father swallows hard.

And then—the truth.

"You were never meant to be born."

Something inside me fractures.

Something inside me splinters.

The words echo, stretch, bleed into the silence.

I exhale. Not a breath. A collapse.

I do not blink.

I do not move.

Because if I move, I will break.

I will shatter like the mirrors in the house I just escaped. I will never be put back together again.

"What?" I whisper. But I already know what she means.

She hesitates, eyes wet, lips trembling. This is not a lie.

Julie clicks her tongue, impatient. "Oh, for God's sake, just say it."

My mother's voice is barely above a whisper. "You were an experiment."

The air is gone. The sky collapses. My pulse roars like a funeral hymn.

My father's voice is hoarse, brittle. "You were never supposed to survive, Rose. You were never supposed to grow up."

My mind fractures.

Julie sighs dramatically, stepping forward, gesturing to me like I am something fascinating, something beautifully tragic. "Your blood" she muses. "It isn't just blood. It's something else. Something they wanted. Something they needed."

I was stolen.

I was stolen for my blood.

I hear Magnus shift, but he does not speak. Dahlia's breath hitches. Daisy, Lily, Clover— they do not move.

And Rhyse—

Rhyse is looking away.

Because she knew.

Because she has always known. The truth is an open wound, festering, bleeding. It spills from my mother's lips like something toxic, like something too heavy to carry.

"They wanted something pure," she says. "Something that could be altered. Something that could be controlled."

Jace's voice is amused. "Something that could be made into something else."

I feel sick.

I feel wrong.

Julie watches me like I am something tragic and beautiful, like I am the moon pulling the tide, like I am a flower she planted only to crush beneath her heel. "You weren't just an experiment, sweetheart. You were the cure."

The words hit me like a knife to the ribs.

"What?" I choke.

Julie shrugs, careless. "They wanted to make something better. They wanted to make something more than human."

I swallow, but the lump in my throat is thick, suffocating. "So they made me?"

Julie grins, tilting her head. "Not made, darling. Designed."

My mind fractures again.

The memories—fragments, pieces of a life that never belonged to me, a past that was not erased but rewritten.

The nights in the cellar. The hunger that never faded. The pain that did not feel like pain but like something burning beneath my skin, like something shifting, changing.

I was not just a prisoner.

I was a creation.

My mother stares at me like she is seeing the ghost of a child she was never meant to love. My father looks away, shame bleeding into the lines on his face.

I do not cry.

I do not move.

Julie sighs, dramatically. "Well, this has been fun, but I think we should probably—"

Magnus moves first.

The gunshot shatters the air.

Julie staggers.

Jace lunges.

And everything erupts.

Blood.

Screams.

The night swallows everything.

I hear my mother cry out.

I hear my father stumble back.

I see Dahlia twist her knife, hear the sound of something breaking.

But all I can see is Rhyse.

She is standing there, watching, frozen.

I know what she is thinking.

I know what she is realizing.

She did not just lose me.

She lost the version of me she thought she was saving.

And maybe—maybe she was never meant to save me at all.

Jace falls.

Julie stumbles.

Kiva is gone.

And I—

I am still here.

My mother reaches for me. "Rose—"

I step back.

I look at my parents, at the people who made me, at the people who abandoned me, at the people who are only here because they want to undo their mistakes.

And I say—

"I am not yours."

Because I am not.

I never was.

I turn to Magnus, to Dahlia, to Daisy, to Lily, to Clover.

To Rhyse.

They are not mine, either.

But they are here.

And maybe—maybe that is enough.

The night is quiet.

The war is not over.

The truth has only just begun to bleed.

But for the first time, I know who I am.

Not a prisoner.

Not an experiment.

Not a daughter lost.

I am something else.

And I will decide what that means.

The wind hums against my skin, carrying the scent of blood and endings. My breath is slow, heavy—but I am still here.

I look at the people who once held me captive. Julie, staggering. Jace, silent. My mother, crying. My father, ashamed.

And for a moment, I wonder—was I ever really theirs?

Was I ever a daughter?

Or was I only ever a design?

A plan made before my first breath, a fate carved into my bones before I could choose my own name.

"Some flowers are born in gardens" I whisper to myself, my voice barely a breath. "Others are planted in graves."

And me?

I was never given a choice.

"Rose" my mother sobs, taking another step forward, but her voice does not belong to me.

It belongs to the child she lost.

The child I am not.

"You don't get to say my name" I murmur. "You don't get to pretend it belongs to you."

Her face crumples. I feel nothing.

Jace exhales, a bitter laugh escaping his lips. "It was never about love" he mutters. "It was about what you could become."

I stare at him, pulse slow, mind burning. They did not love me.

They created me.

Like hands sculpting clay, carving me into something useful, something they could use, something they could control.

Julie grins, despite the blood staining her lips. "And you became so much more than we ever imagined."

I tighten my grip on the knife in my hand.

"Then let me show you what I have become."

The past stands before me, hands outstretched.

The future stands behind me, waiting to be taken.

And Rhyse—Rhyse stands beside me, silent.

For the first time, she is not pulling me back.

She is letting me choose.

I inhale, slow.

"I do not forgive you" I say.

My mother's face twists. My father flinches.

"But I will not carry you with me, either."

Because ghosts only follow you if you let them.

And I am done being haunted.

I turn my back to them, stepping into the cold night, into the unknown.

Julie does not stop me.

Jace does not stop me.

Even my mother does not call out my name again.

Because they know—

I do not belong to them anymore.

And for the first time, I am free.

The wind whispers secrets against my skin, but I do not listen. The past is behind me, broken, bleeding, desperate to be remembered, but I do not turn around. The night stretches endlessly before me, and for the first time, I do not fear it. The hush inside me is quiet, waiting, watching, no longer dragging me backward but stepping forward with me, as if it, too, has been freed. My fingers ache from holding weapons I should have never had to hold, my ribs feel hollow from years of hunger—hunger for truth, hunger for answers, hunger for something that no longer matters. The stars above blink, but they do not care for the wars fought beneath them. The world does not pause for grief, for revelation, for the child who was stolen and the woman who walked away.

Rhyse is beside me, silent, but this silence is different now. It is not the silence of secrets, not the silence of betrayal. It is the silence of understanding, of something unspoken between us, something heavier than words. She does not ask me if I am okay. She knows I am not. She does not tell me we did the right thing. She knows right and wrong were never part of this story. The others follow, Dahlia clutching her knife like a promise, Daisy shaking but steady, Magnus watching me as if I am something fragile but refusing to treat me as such. They do not fill the night with questions. They do not try to fix something that cannot be fixed. Instead, they walk.

And then, Rhyse speaks. "What now?" Her voice is quiet, as if she already knows there is no answer. I do not stop walking. "We end it." I do not know what that means, but I know that we cannot keep running, cannot keep looking over our shoulders, waiting for the past to catch up. The past is already here. It has always been here. And the only way to stop it is to face it. Magnus exhales, slow. "Julie and Jace won't disappear." "I don't want them to," I say. "I want them to see me." To see what they created, what they broke, what they could never truly own.

The night presses in, but I do not bend beneath it. My blood was never mine, but my choices are. The flowers they tried to grow in the dark have cracked through the stone, have reached for the light despite the hands that buried them. And I—I will not wither.

The road ahead is endless, stretching like a wound torn open across the earth. The air tastes of endings, of something old unraveling, of something waiting to be buried. The past does not chase me anymore, because I am no longer running. My feet move forward, one step, then another, but the weight inside me is heavier than ever. I have spent years searching for answers, clawing at the walls of my mind, desperate to remember, desperate to know. And now that I do, it does not feel like relief. It feels like rot. Like something curling around my bones, whispering that I was never meant to escape, that my story was written long before I had the chance to hold the pen.

Rhyse walks beside me, her presence quiet but no longer distant. The betrayal still lingers between us, a wound that will never fully heal, but there is something else now too—a grief we share. She has lost something tonight. Maybe she has lost everything. And yet, she has never looked more free. The weight of pretending is gone, the mask has cracked, and in its place, there is only the girl who was left behind the same way I was. We are not the same, but we are not so different either. I do not forgive her, but I do not leave her behind. Maybe that is enough.

Magnus is ahead, his pace steady, his gaze sharp. He has always known more than he says, carried more than he lets on. I wonder if he has been waiting for this moment, if he has been waiting for me to see the world as it is, for me to stop asking questions that have no good answers. He glances at me, and for the first time, he does not look at me like I am something broken. He looks at me like he is waiting to see what I will do next.

Julie and Jace will not disappear. They will find another way, another game, another child to shape into something unnatural. Unless I stop them. Unless I finish what they started.

The thought is a whisper in my mind, curling like smoke, wrapping around my ribs. It does not scare me. It does not feel like something wicked or wrong. It feels like clarity.

We reach the edge of the city, where the lights dim, where the world grows quiet. The stars blink overhead, unaware, uninterested. The night does not care for me. But I do not need it to.

I stop walking.

Daisy shifts beside me, her fingers twitching like she wants to reach for me, but she doesn't. Dahlia watches, waiting, unreadable as always. Clover murmurs something to Lily, who only nods. The silence between us is thick, humming with things none of us are ready to say.

Then, Rhyse speaks. "What now?"

I exhale, slow, steady. For the first time, I know the answer.

"Now," I say, turning to face them, "we burn it all down."

The hush inside me does not fight me this time.

Because for the first time, it is not trying to pull me back.

It is pushing me forward.

Chapter XI

My Eleven Years

Suddenly it has been a heavy wave of betrayal and change over my roots, I want to stay quiet and loud only to my diary for some days.

Dear Diary

December 1st

The cold bites at my skin, the air crisp with winter's hush. The world is quieter now, as if waiting for something to end, something to begin.

It has been weeks since I walked away, since I let the past crumble behind me like ruins too broken to rebuild. I am still trying to understand what that means. What it means to live for myself.

For eleven years, I have been running, breaking, surviving. But survival is not the same as living. Survival is hunger without fulfillment, breath without purpose, motion without meaning. And I want more.

I do not know where I belong. I do not know if I belong anywhere. But maybe that is the point. Maybe some flowers are not meant to stay rooted in one place. Maybe some are meant to scatter, to grow wild, to bloom wherever the wind carries them.

I was never given a home. So I will make one in myself.

Dear Diary

December 5th

Rhyse walks beside me, our footprints vanishing behind us, swallowed by the falling snow. She does not ask where we are going. She does not tell me she is sorry again. She just stays.

She has always been quiet, but this silence is different now. It is no longer a silence of secrets, of things left unsaid. It is the silence of two people learning how to exist outside of cages.

She told me once that she never knew her own birthday. Julie never told her. Jace never celebrated it. Her name was never written on a cake, never whispered in the hush of a wish.

"Then pick one," I told her. "Any day you want."

She thought for a moment, then shrugged. "December 11th."

I blinked. "That's my birthday."

Her lips curled slightly, the closest thing to a smile she has ever given me. "Then I guess it's mine too."

And just like that, she took something that had always felt lonely and made it ours.

Dear Diary

December 11th

I turn eighteen today. At least, I think I do.

I have no birth certificate, no proof, only my own calculations, my own whispered counting in the dark. Seven years with my real parents. Eleven years in the cellar. Seven plus eleven is eighteen.

But I do not feel eighteen.

I feel ancient. I feel like something that has lived a thousand lives, died a thousand deaths. I feel like something that should not still be standing, and yet, here I am.

Rhyse and Magnus find an old café, the kind with foggy windows and creaky wooden chairs, and they sit me down as if this day matters. As if I matter. Magnus places a candle in the center of the table, lights it with the flick of his wrist. "Happy birthday, kid," he says, voice rough but warm.

I stare at the flickering flame, feeling something unfamiliar creep into my chest.

I have never celebrated a birthday. Not with cake, not with gifts, not with anything but the bitter taste of time passing without permission.

And yet, here we are.

It is small. But it is real.

For the first time in my life, I close my eyes and make a wish.

I do not wish to go back. I do not wish for the past to be rewritten.

I simply wish to keep walking.

Dear Diary

December 15th

We find an old bookstore, the kind that smells like dust and forgotten words. I run my fingers over the spines, feeling the weight of every story I have never been allowed to read. Stories of people who existed before me. Stories of people who were allowed to be more than just what they were made to be.

I pick up a book about flowers. Not because I care about botany, but because I care about what it means to grow.

There is a passage that catches my eye.

"Some flowers are planted in sunlight. Others are buried in the dark. But no matter where they begin, they all bloom toward the same sky."

I trace the words, something twisting inside me.

I think of Daisy, Dahlia, Clover, Lily. Flowers given names but never given a chance. I think of Rhyse, whose name was never a flower at all. I think of myself, a flower stolen from its roots before it ever had the chance to bloom.

And yet, we are still here.

Dear Diary

December 20th

The snow falls heavier now, blanketing the world in white, covering the past like something that begs to be buried. But I do not forget.

Julie and Jace are still out there. Kiva is still watching from the shadows. The past does not let go so easily.

But I do not fear them anymore.

Let them come. Let them watch. Let them see what they tried to break and failed to destroy. I will not run.

Dear Diary

December 25th

Christmas means nothing to me. It never has.

Holidays are just dates on a calendar, moments other people have given meaning. But to me, they have always been just another day to survive.

But this year, something is different.

Rhyse finds an abandoned house, Magnus finds firewood, Dahlia finds a broken radio that somehow still hums a song. Daisy hands me an old coat, tells me to take it before I freeze.

And for the first time, I think—maybe this is what family feels like.

Not blood. Not obligation.

Just presence.

Dear Diary

December 31st

The year ends.

I am still here.

I have lost everything. I have gained something I do not yet understand. But for the first time, I do not dread what comes next.

The past is gone. The future is waiting.

And I am walking toward it.

Dear Diary

January 1st

I wake up to a sunrise.

I have never paid attention to them before.

But today, I do.

The sky is bleeding into gold, the light touching everything it can reach. It is quiet. It is beautiful.

It is a beginning.

And I smile.

Because for the first time in my life, I am not just surviving.

I am alive.

"Some flowers bloom early. Some take time. Some are cut before they ever get the chance. But even in the darkest soil, even in the coldest winter, even in the most unlikely places, something always grows."

I was sent to bloom, but never could.

But it is never too late.

And now, I will bloom on my own terms.

I will bloom, and no one will ever cut me down again.

Dear Diary

January 2nd

The cold is sharper today, sinking through my skin like teeth. The world is still, the wind whispering through the abandoned streets as if carrying the echoes of ghosts who refuse to leave. I press my fingers to my ribs, feeling the sharpness beneath. My body has always felt like a collection of jagged edges, like something unfinished. But maybe that's what survival is learning to live with the pieces that never quite fit.

Rhyse watches me from the steps of the house we've claimed for the night. She doesn't speak, but her silence no longer feels like a cage. It feels like a question. One she is afraid to ask, one I am afraid to answer.

"Are we really free?"

I do not know.

Maybe freedom is not a door you walk through, but a weight you learn to carry.

Dear Diary

January 5th

Magnus tells me that sometimes, the best thing you can do is walk away. That not every battle is meant to be fought, that sometimes, the war is surviving in spite of everything. I listen, but I do not agree.

Julie and Jace still breathe. Kiva still waits in the shadows. The past does not vanish because I chose to leave it behind. It lingers, it festers, it watches from the corners of my mind.

And I cannot let it rot there.

"You want to go back," Rhyse says, reading my thoughts before I can even speak them.

I nod. "Not to stay. To end it."

She exhales, slow, steady. "Then I'll go with you."

There is something in her eyes I do not recognize, something fragile, something almost human.

"Why?" I ask.

She hesitates. "Because I need to know if I was ever real."

The words cut through the air like a blade. I do not ask what she means. I think I already know.

She was raised to be a ghost, just like I was.

Dear Diary

January 7th

I wake up gasping.

The dream was different this time. No cellar, no chains, no hands pulling me back into the dark.

This time, I was standing in a field. The flowers were wilting, their petals curling inward, their roots strangling the earth beneath them. I reached out to touch one, and it crumbled beneath my fingertips, turning to dust. The wind carried it away, scattering it into nothingness.

And then, a voice.

"You were never meant to bloom."

I turned, but there was no one there. Only shadows. Only echoes.

When I woke, the words still clung to my skin like dirt.

I press my hand against my heart, feeling the slow, steady beat beneath my ribs.

"But I did."

Dear Diary

January 10th

We find an old motel on the outskirts of town, its neon sign flickering, buzzing like a dying insect. It smells like dust and forgotten things, like stories left unfinished. I sit on the edge of the bed, staring at my hands.

Rhyse sits beside me, silent. I know she is remembering too.

Julie never let her have a name of a flower. She was always just Rhyse. No petals, no softness, nothing delicate.

"You think she did it on purpose?" I ask, breaking the silence.

She doesn't look at me. "Maybe she knew I was never meant to grow."

The words are quiet, but they settle heavy between us.

I shake my head. "That's not true."

Rhyse exhales, running a hand through her tangled hair. "Isn't it? I was always the one who watched. I was always the one who kept you where you were supposed to be. Maybe I wasn't meant to bloom because I was never supposed to leave the garden."

I look at her, really look at her. She is tired, she is thin, she is carrying something so heavy I can almost feel it pressing against my own ribs.

She was never a flower. But maybe that's because she was never given the chance.

Maybe we were all trapped in the same garden. Some of us just didn't realize it until it was too late.

Dear Diary

January 12th

I sit outside in the cold, watching the breath curl from my lips like smoke.

It has been eleven years. Eleven years of questions, of hunger, of waiting for a life that was never coming. I thought I would feel different now, now that I know the truth. But the truth does not change the past. It does not erase the scars. It does not fill the hollow spaces inside me.

It only names them.

And I do not know if that is enough.

Daisy sits beside me, pulling her coat tighter around her frame. "You think too much," she murmurs.

I smirk, but it is hollow. "That's what happens when you have nothing else to do."

She is quiet for a long time. Then—

"You're my sister."

The words are soft, almost lost to the wind.

I inhale sharply, my chest tightening. I do not know how to respond.

I think of my mother, the woman who gave birth to me but never fought to keep me. I think of Julie, the woman who raised me but never loved me. And then I think of Daisy, sitting beside me in the cold, telling me I am something to her.

"I don't know how to be that," I admit.

She shrugs. "Me neither."

And somehow, that is enough.

Dear Diary

January 15th

We leave the motel before dawn, the sky still heavy with sleep. My ribs ache with something I cannot name. My hands are steady, but my pulse is wild.

I do not know where we are g

I do not know if we are running toward something or away from it.

But I know one thing.

I am not afraid.

Some flowers are planted in sunlight. Some are buried in darkness. Some bloom early, some bloom late, and some never bloom at all.

I was not given a garden. I was not given sunlight, or warmth, or the gentle hands that coax petals open. I was given a cage. I was given silence. I was given a world that told me I was never meant to grow.

But still, I did.

And I will keep growing.

Because it is never too late to bloom.

The night stretches endlessly, swallowing time, swallowing words. The wind hums through the abandoned streets, carrying echoes of a past that refuses to rest. Snowflakes kiss the earth, soft and fleeting, vanishing the moment they touch the ground. A reminder that not everything meant to stay will.

Rose stands at the edge of the city, the cold biting at her skin, but she does not move. The weight of the last eleven years presses against her ribs, but for the first time, she does not try to escape it. Some wounds are not meant to be healed. Some are meant to be carried.

Behind her, Rhyse watches in silence. Not as a shadow, not as a captor, not as a ghost tied to another's existence. But as something new, something uncertain, something free. They are not the same, but they are not so different either. Two lost things, learning how to exist in a world that never made space for them.

Daisy, Dahlia, Lily, and Clover stand nearby, their faces unreadable, their fates uncertain. They were all stolen, all forgotten, all left to wither in a place where nothing was meant to grow. But they are not dead. And as long as something still breathes, it can still bloom.

Magnus lingers in the background, his expression carved from something tired and knowing. He does not ask what comes next. He does not need to. This has never been his story to finish.

And Rose, she finally understands.

There is no going back. Not to her real parents, who lost her long before she was taken. Not to

Julie and Jace, who tried to shape her into something unrecognizable. Not to the past, not to the cellar, not to the girl she used to be.

She does not belong to any of them.

She belongs to herself.

The snow crunches beneath her boots as she turns, her gaze steady, her voice calm. "Let's go."

No hesitation. No fear.

Because the story does not end in survival.

It ends in choice.

And for the first time in eleven years, she chooses herself.

The road ahead is unknown, stretching into a silence that no longer feels empty. It is not safety. It is not certainty. It is not the warmth of a home she once dreamed of. But it is hers.

Rose looks at the faces around her, Rhyse, who was never meant to leave but did. Daisy, who carries the same blood but not the same memories. Dahlia, Lily, and Clover, each a flower that never had the chance to bloom. Magnus, who has always been more of a father than the one who made her.

They are not whole. They are not healed. But they are here. And that is enough.

The past will not change. It will not soften its edges to make space for them. It will remain cruel and unrelenting, a garden of wilted flowers that will never bloom again.

But they are not the past.

They are what comes after.

Rose exhales, watching the warmth of her breath dissolve into the cold. The scars on her skin do not fade, the weight in her chest does not lift, but something within her shifts; subtle, quiet, powerful.

Not everything broken needs to be fixed. Some things are meant to be carried.

She steps forward.

And this time, she does not look back.

The snow keeps falling, soft and relentless, burying footprints before they have the chance to last. The world does not pause for them. It never has. It only moves forward, indifferent to who is left behind.

Rose does not know what awaits her beyond this night, beyond this moment. There is no perfect ending, no promise of peace, no certainty that the scars won't ache when the cold settles in. But she knows this, she will not wither where she was planted.

She was not given sunlight. She was not given warmth. She was left in the dark, expected to break, expected to rot. But some flowers do not die in the absence of light. Some flowers learn to bloom in the dark, with roots so deep that no storm can tear them from the earth.

She tightens her coat around her, feeling the wind whisper against her skin. The others are waiting. The past is behind her. The future is unwritten.

And then, in a voice as steady as the ground beneath her feet, she speaks the truth she has always known but never dared to say—

"They sent us to bloom, but never let us. And now, they expect us to die. But I have learned something, flowers do not ask for permission to grow. They break through stone. They crack the earth open. And no matter how many times they are cut, they always, always find a way back to the sun."

And with that, she walks forward, leaving behind the ghosts, the chains, the names that were never truly hers.

Because she is not a girl in a garden anymore.

She is the storm that will make it bloom.